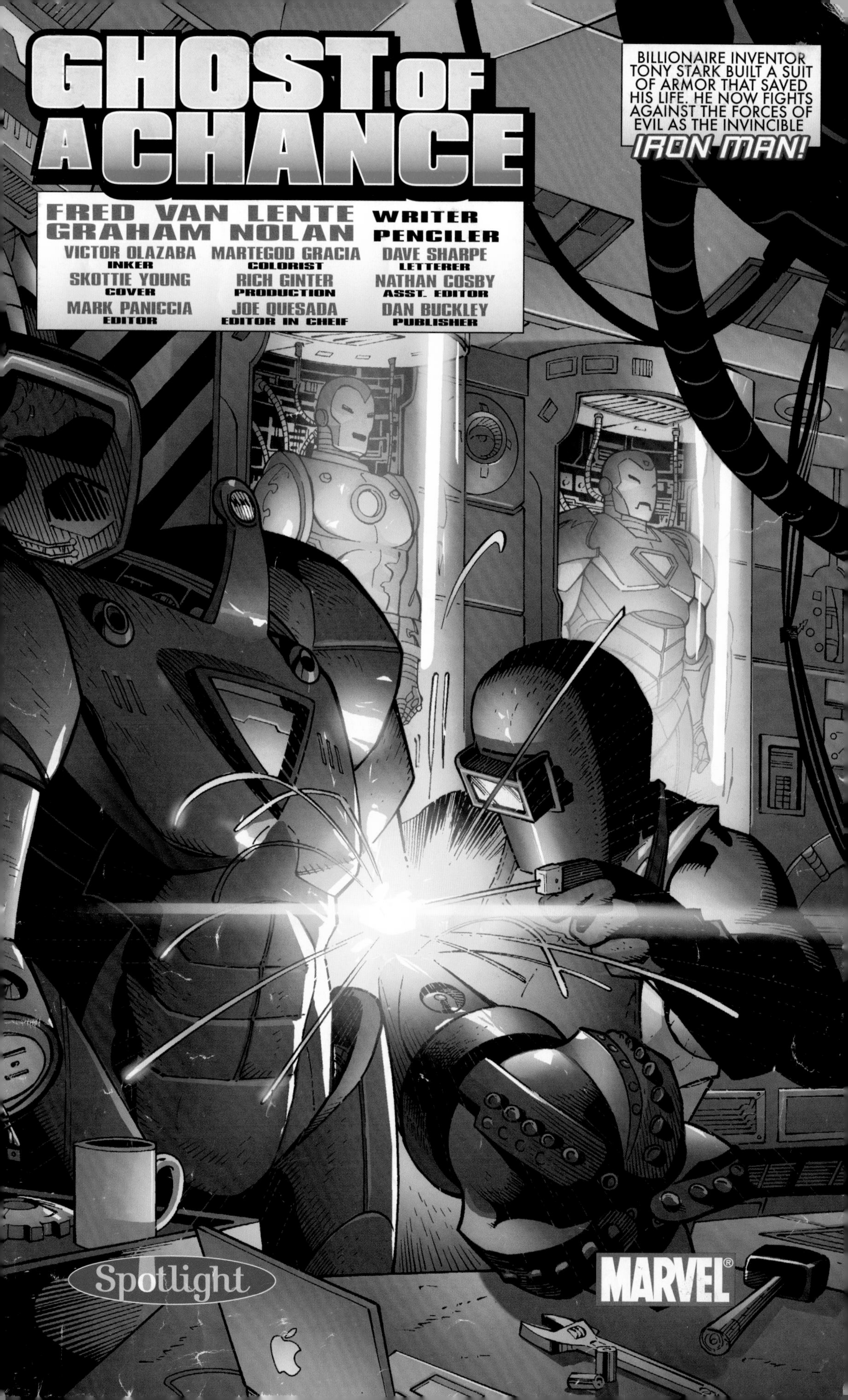
GHOST OF A CHANCE
BILLIONAIRE INVENTOR TONY STARK BUILT A SUIT OF ARMOR THAT SAVED HIS LIFE. HE NOW FIGHTS AGAINST THE FORCES OF EVIL AS THE INVINCIBLE IRON MAN!
FRED VAN LENTE WRITER
GRAHAM NOLAN PENCILER
VICTOR OLAZABA INKER
MARTEGOD GRACIA COLORIST
DAVE SHARPE LETTERER
SKOTTIE YOUNG COVER
RICH GINTER PRODUCTION
NATHAN COSBY ASST. EDITOR
MARK PANICCIA EDITOR
JOE QUESADA EDITOR IN CHEIF
DAN BUCKLEY PUBLISHER
Spotlight
MARVEL®

VISIT US AT
www.abdopublishing.com

Reinforced library bound edition published in 2009 by Spotlight, a division of the ABDO Group, 8000 West 78th Street, Edina, Minnesota 55439. Spotlight produces high-quality reinforced library bound editions for schools and libraries. Published by agreement with Marvel Characters, Inc.

Library of Congress Cataloging-in-Publication Data

Van Lente, Fred.
  Ghost of a chance / Fred Van Lente, writer ; Graham Nolan, penciler ; Victor Olazaba, inker ; Martegod Gracia, colorist ; Dave Sharpe, letterer ; Skottie Young, cover. -- Reinforced library bound ed.
     p. cm. -- (Iron Man)
  "Marvel."
  ISBN 978-1-59961-590-5
  1. Graphic novels. [1. Graphic novels. 2. Superheroes--Fiction.] I. Nolan, Graham, ill. II. Title.
  PZ7.7.V26Gh 2009
  [Fic]--dc22

                    2008033396

All Spotlight books have reinforced library bindings and are manufactured in the United States of America.

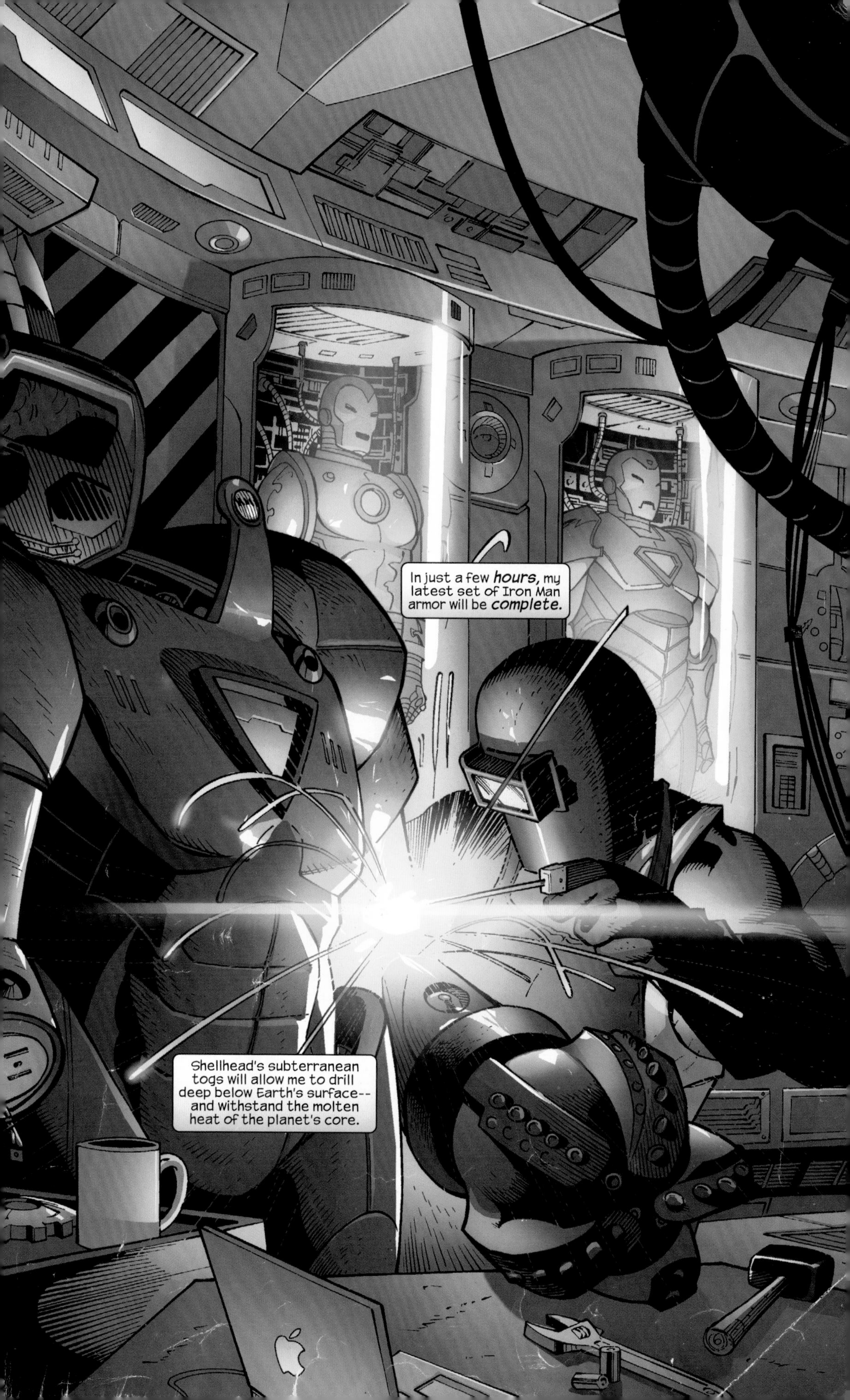
In just a few **hours,** my latest set of Iron Man armor will be ***complete.***
Shellhead's subterranean togs will allow me to drill deep below Earth's surface-- and withstand the molten heat of the planet's core.

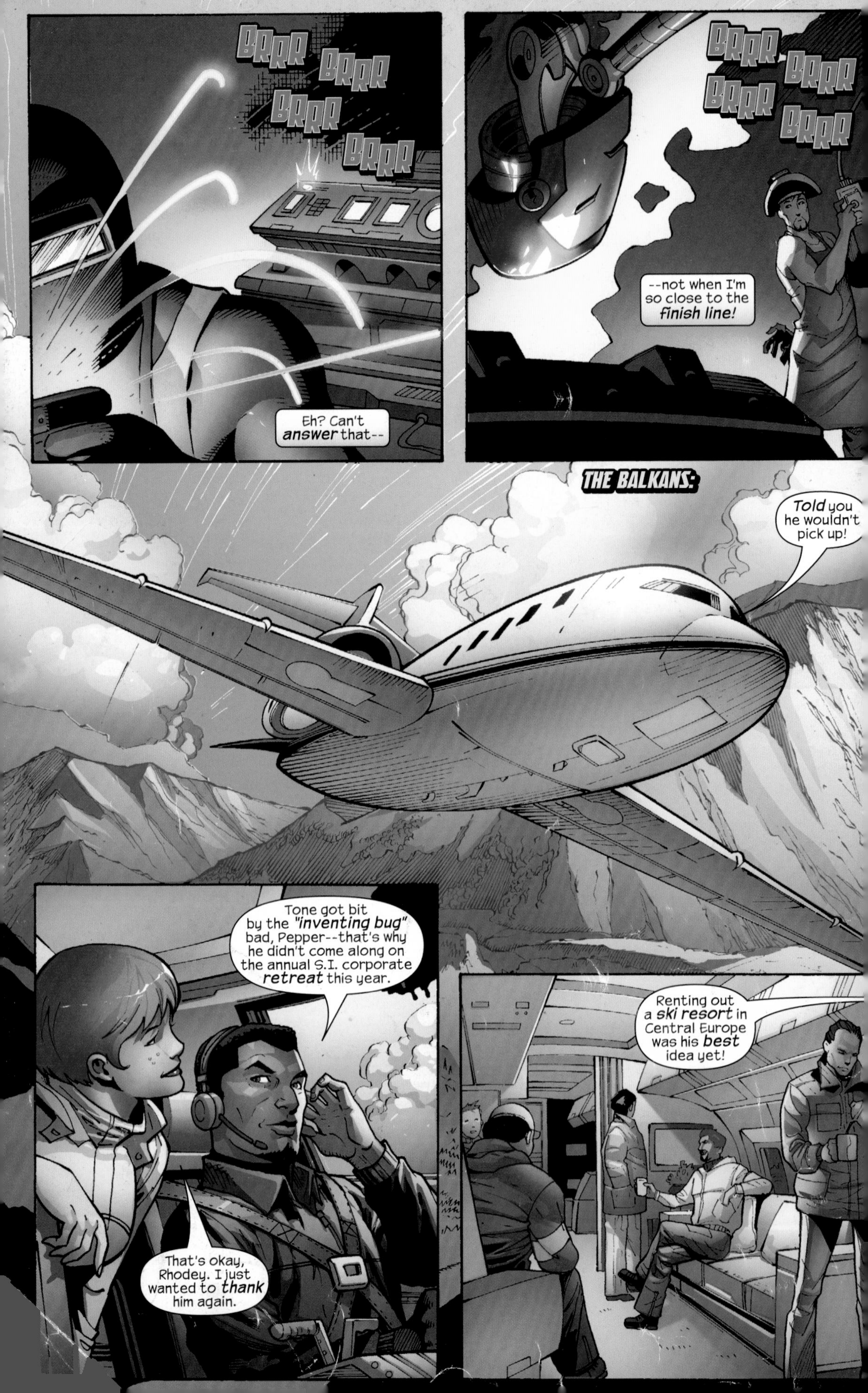
BRRR BRRR BRRR BRRR
Eh? Can't *answer* that--
BRRR BRRR BRRR BRRR
--not when I'm so close to the *finish line!*
THE BALKANS:
Told you he wouldn't pick up!
Tone got bit by the *"inventing bug"* bad, Pepper--that's why he didn't come along on the annual S.I. corporate *retreat* this year.
That's okay, Rhodey. I just wanted to *thank* him again.
Renting out a *ski resort* in Central Europe was his *best* idea yet!

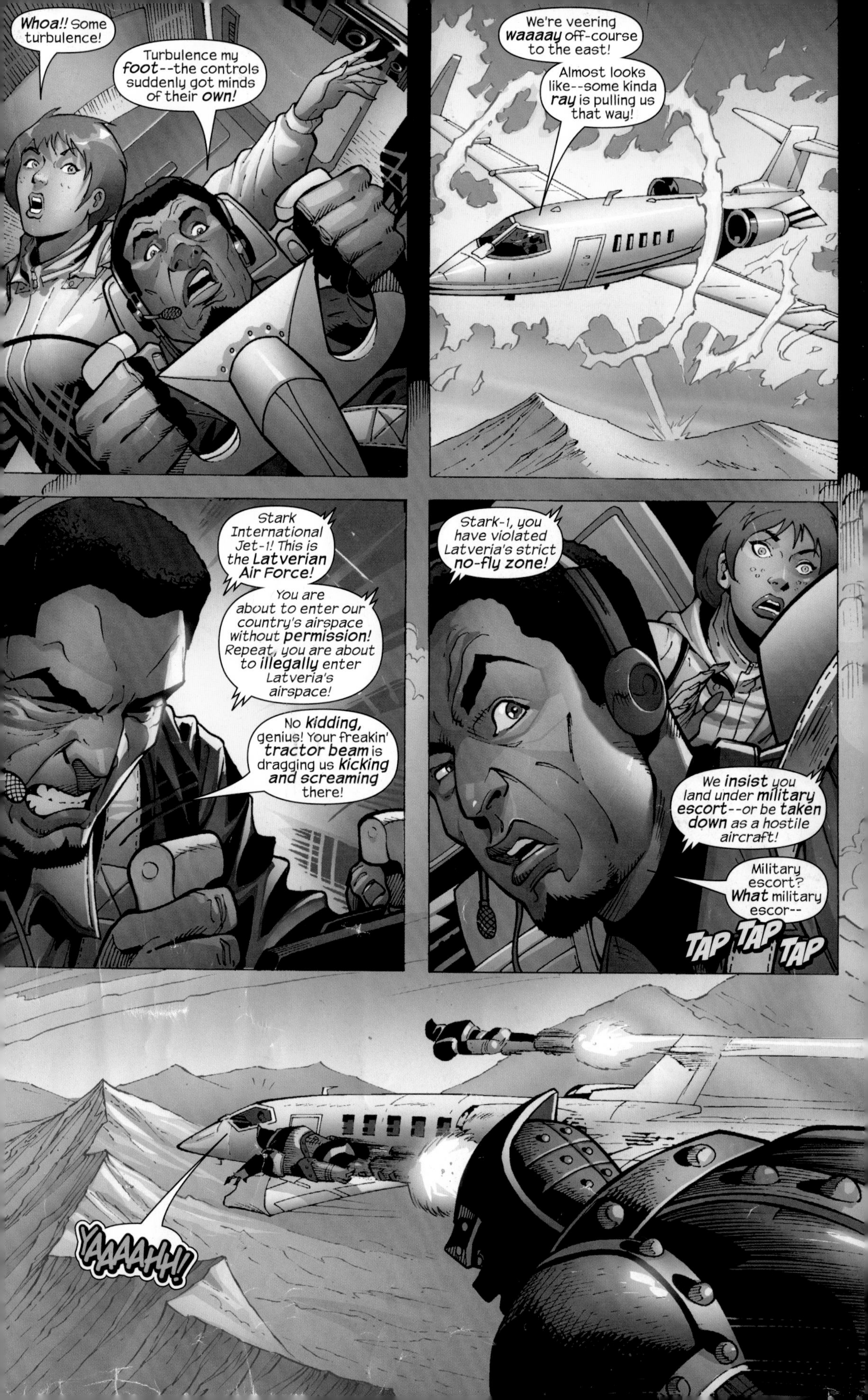

Whoa!! Some turbulence!
Turbulence my foot--the controls suddenly got minds of their own!
We're veering waaaay off-course to the east!
Almost looks like--some kinda ray is pulling us that way!
Stark International Jet-1! This is the Latverian Air Force!
You are about to enter our country's airspace without permission! Repeat, you are about to illegally enter Latveria's airspace!
No kidding, genius! Your freakin' tractor beam is dragging us kicking and screaming there!
Stark-1, you have violated Latveria's strict no-fly zone!
We insist you land under military escort--or be taken down as a hostile aircraft!
Military escort? What military escor--
TAP TAP TAP
YAAAAHH!!

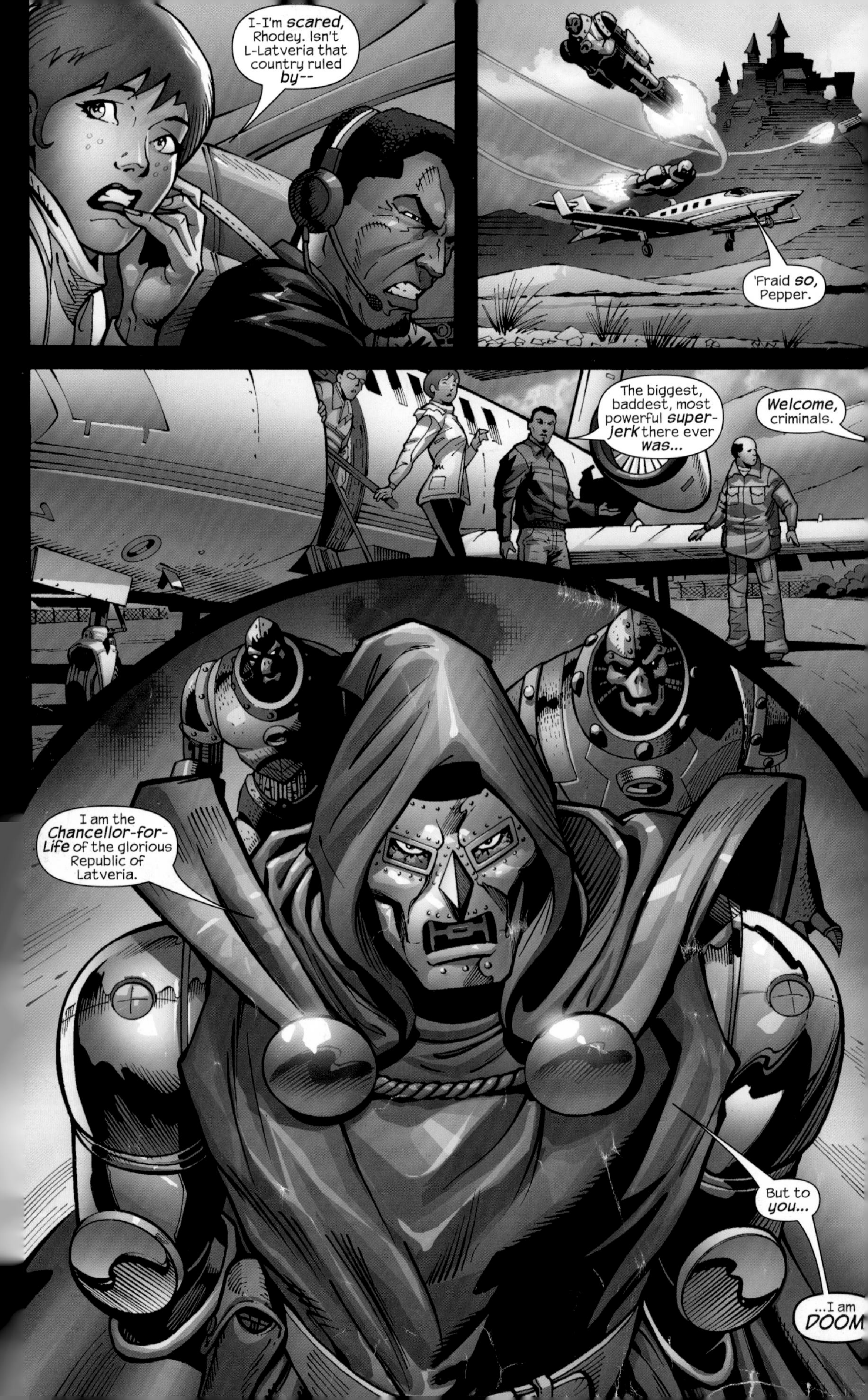
I-I'm scared, Rhodey. Isn't L-Latveria that country ruled by--
'Fraid so, Pepper.
The biggest, baddest, most powerful super-jerk there ever was...
Welcome, criminals.
I am the Chancellor-for-Life of the glorious Republic of Latveria.
But to you...
...I am DOOM

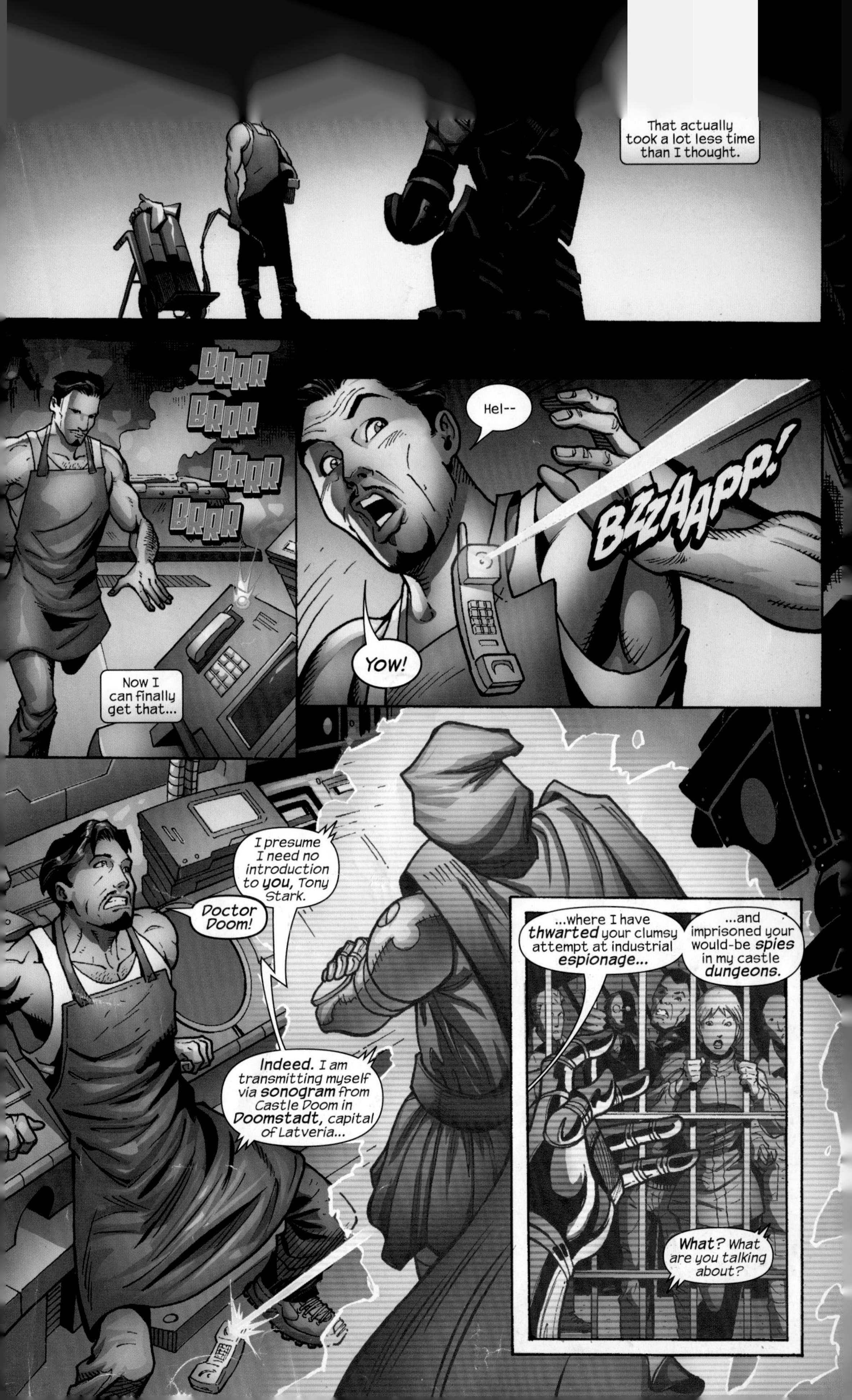
That actually took a lot less time than I thought.
BRRR BRRR BRRR BRRR
Now I can finally get that...
Hel--
BZZAAPP!
YOW!
I presume I need no introduction to you, Tony Stark.
Doctor Doom!
Indeed. I am transmitting myself via sonogram from Castle Doom in Doomstadt, capital of Latveria...
...where I have thwarted your clumsy attempt at industrial espionage...
...and imprisoned your would-be spies in my castle dungeons.
What? What are you talking about?

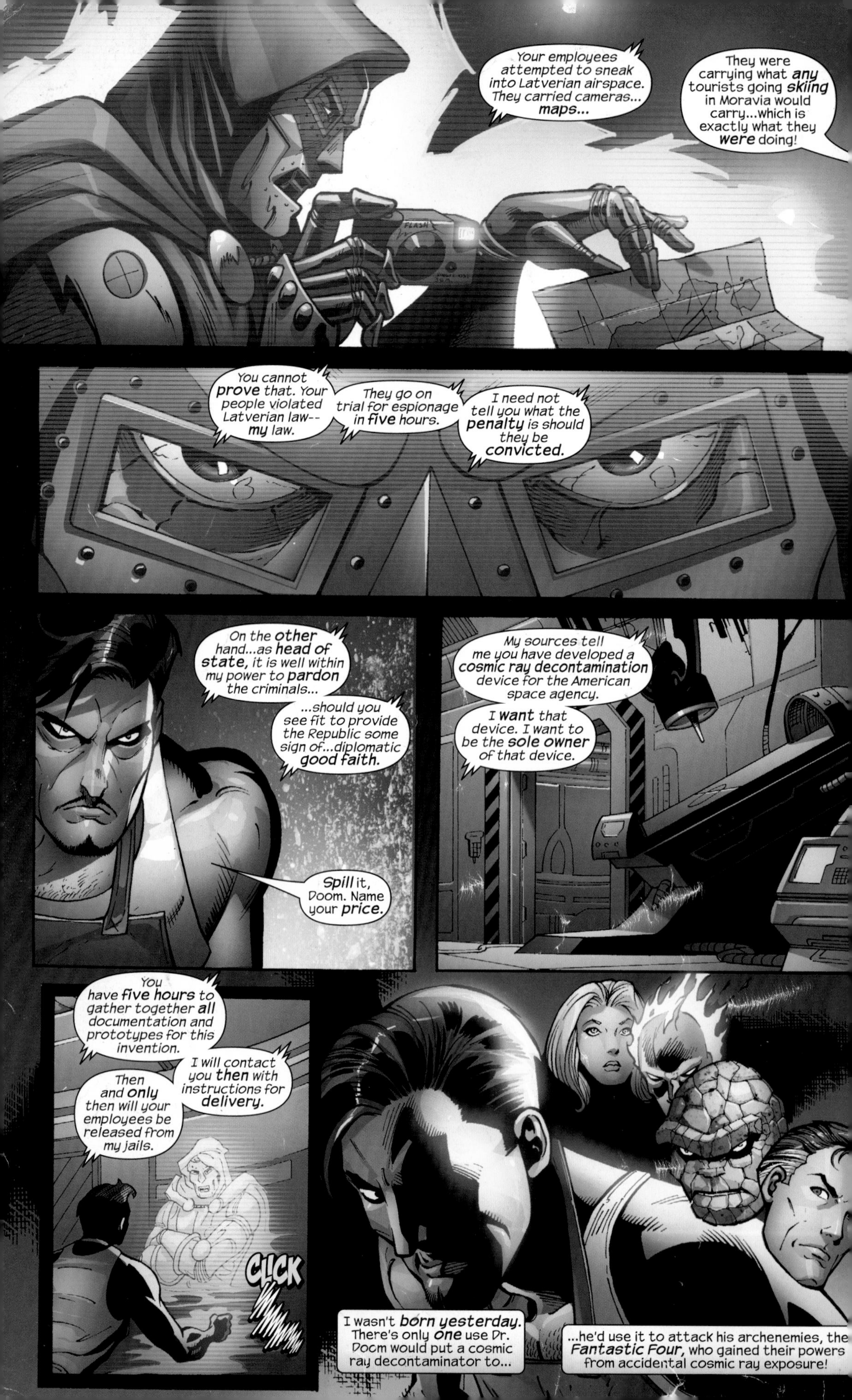
Your employees attempted to sneak into Latverian airspace. They carried cameras... maps...
They were carrying what any tourists going skiing in Moravia would carry...which is exactly what they were doing!
You cannot prove that. Your people violated Latverian law-- my law.
They go on trial for espionage in five hours.
I need not tell you what the penalty is should they be convicted.
On the other hand...as head of state, it is well within my power to pardon the criminals...
...should you see fit to provide the Republic some sign of...diplomatic good faith.
Spill it, Doom. Name your price.
My sources tell me you have developed a cosmic ray decontamination device for the American space agency.
I want that device. I want to be the sole owner of that device.
You have five hours to gather together all documentation and prototypes for this invention.
I will contact you then with instructions for delivery.
Then and only then will your employees be released from my jails.
CLICK
I wasn't born yesterday. There's only one use Dr. Doom would put a cosmic ray decontaminator to...
...he'd use it to attack his archenemies, the Fantastic Four, who gained their powers from accidental cosmic ray exposure!

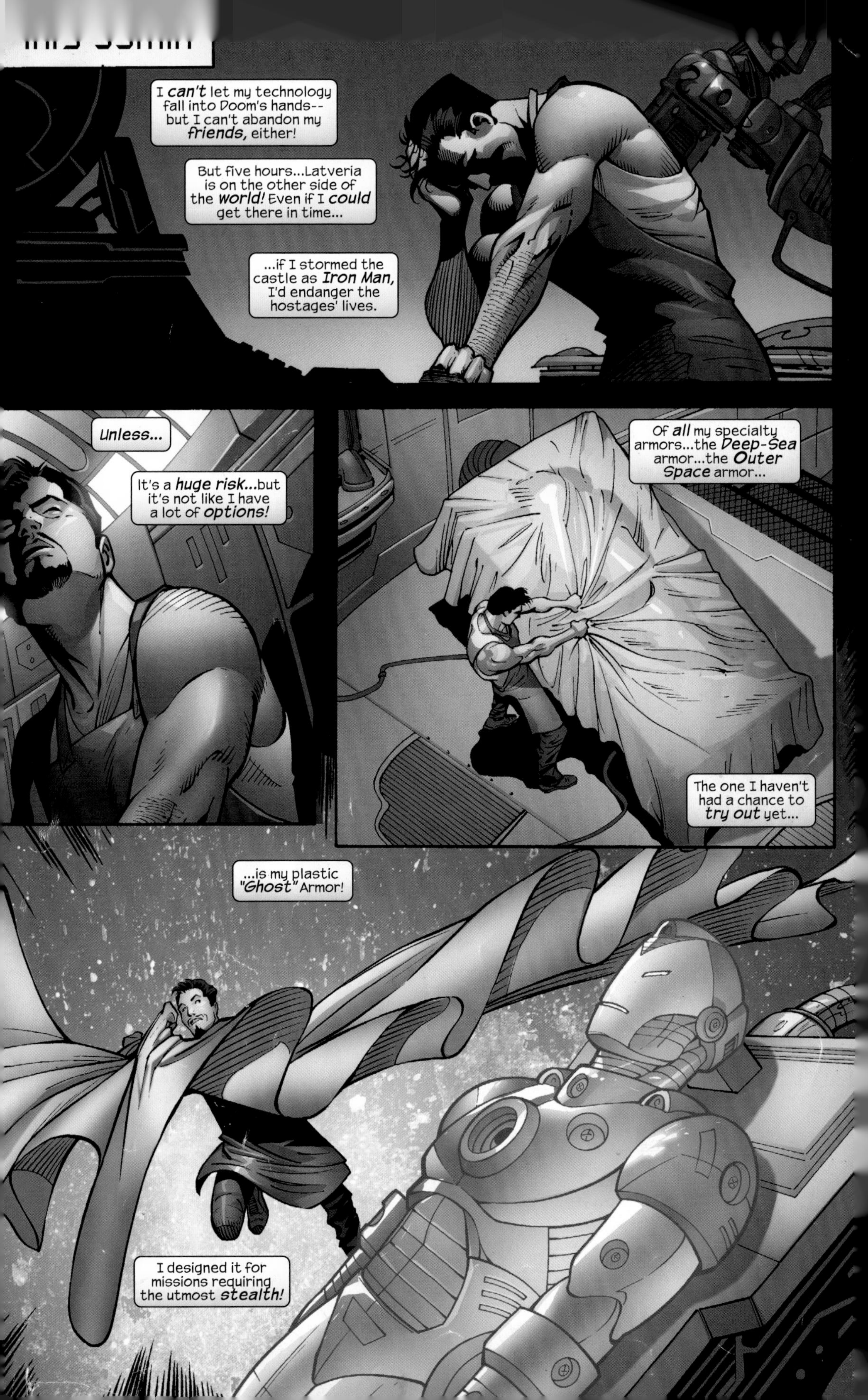

I can't let my technology fall into Doom's hands--but I can't abandon my friends, either!
But five hours...Latveria is on the other side of the world! Even if I could get there in time...
...if I stormed the castle as Iron Man, I'd endanger the hostages' lives.
Unless...
It's a huge risk...but it's not like I have a lot of options!
Of all my specialty armors...the Deep-Sea armor...the Outer Space armor...
The one I haven't had a chance to try out yet...
...is my plastic "Ghost" Armor!
I designed it for missions requiring the utmost stealth!

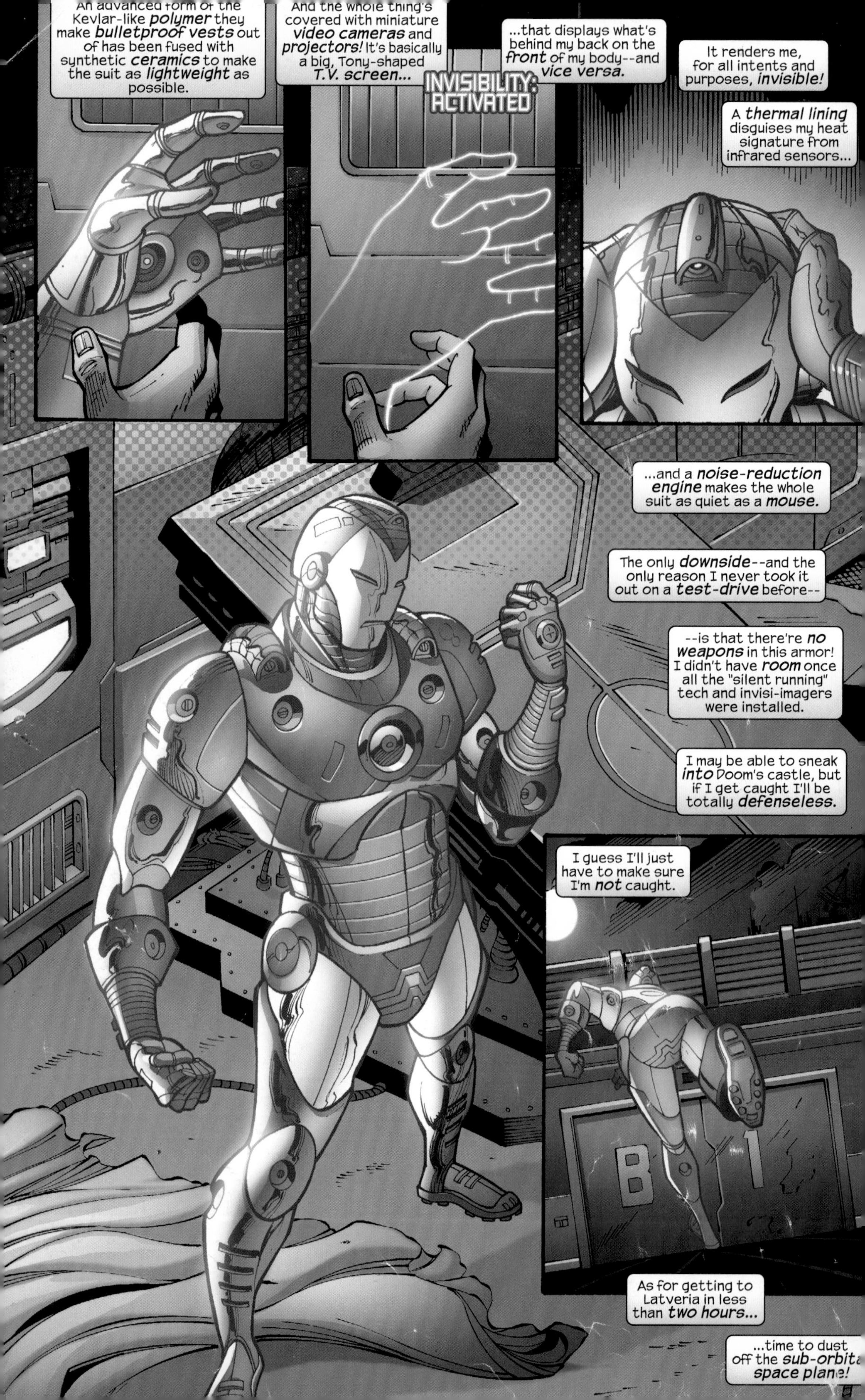
An advanced form of the Kevlar-like polymer they make bulletproof vests out of has been fused with synthetic ceramics to make the suit as lightweight as possible.
And the whole thing's covered with miniature video cameras and projectors! It's basically a big, Tony-shaped T.V. screen...
INVISIBILITY: ACTIVATED
...that displays what's behind my back on the front of my body--and vice versa.
It renders me, for all intents and purposes, invisible!
A thermal lining disguises my heat signature from infrared sensors...
...and a noise-reduction engine makes the whole suit as quiet as a mouse.
The only downside--and the only reason I never took it out on a test-drive before--
--is that there're no weapons in this armor! I didn't have room once all the "silent running" tech and invisi-imagers were installed.
I may be able to sneak into Doom's castle, but if I get caught I'll be totally defenseless.
I guess I'll just have to make sure I'm not caught.
B 1
As for getting to Latveria in less than two hours...
...time to dust off the sub-orbit space plane!

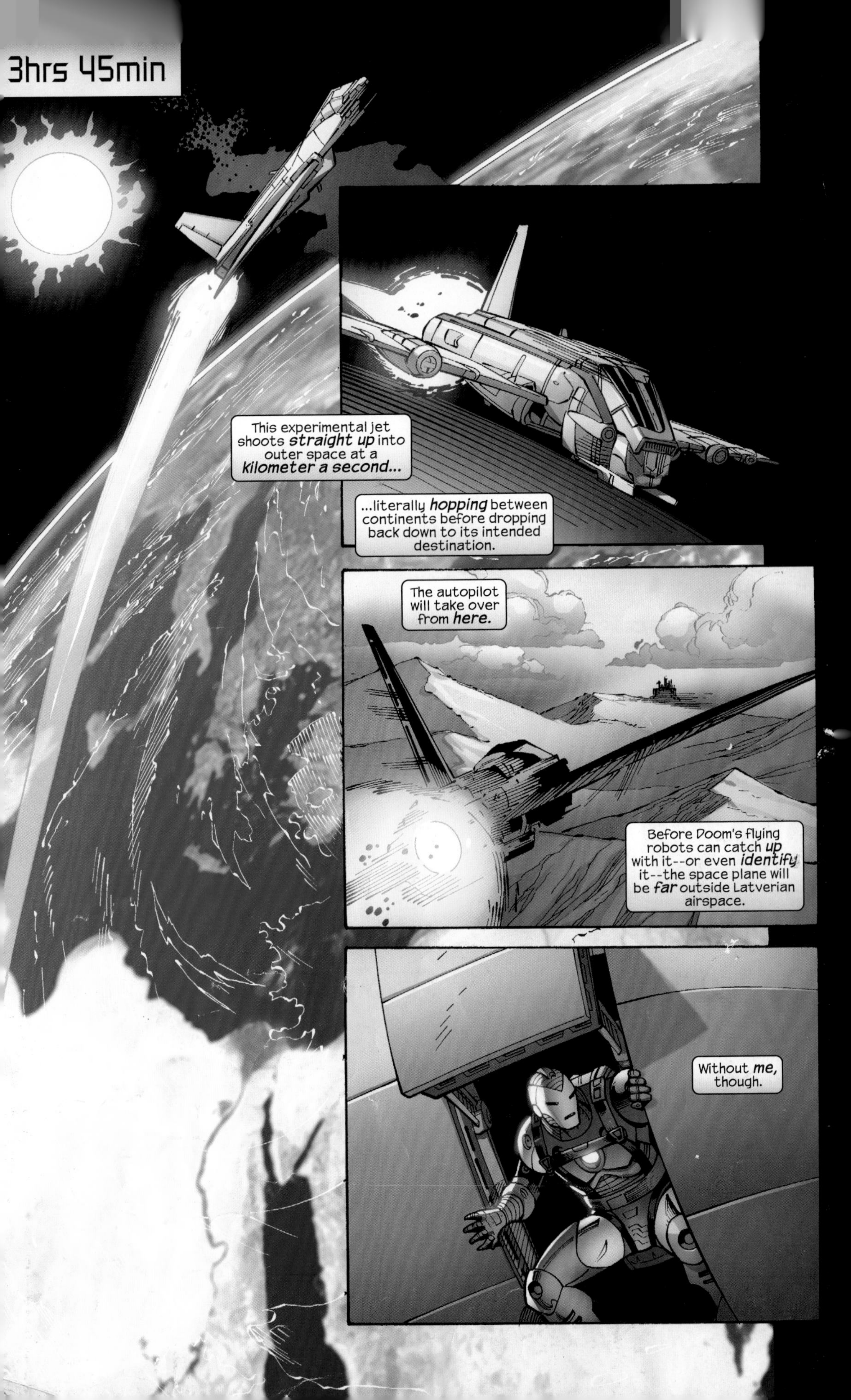
3hrs 45min
This experimental jet shoots straight up into outer space at a kilometer a second...
...literally hopping between continents before dropping back down to its intended destination.
The autopilot will take over from here.
Before Doom's flying robots can catch up with it--or even identify it--the space plane will be far outside Latverian airspace.
Without me, though.

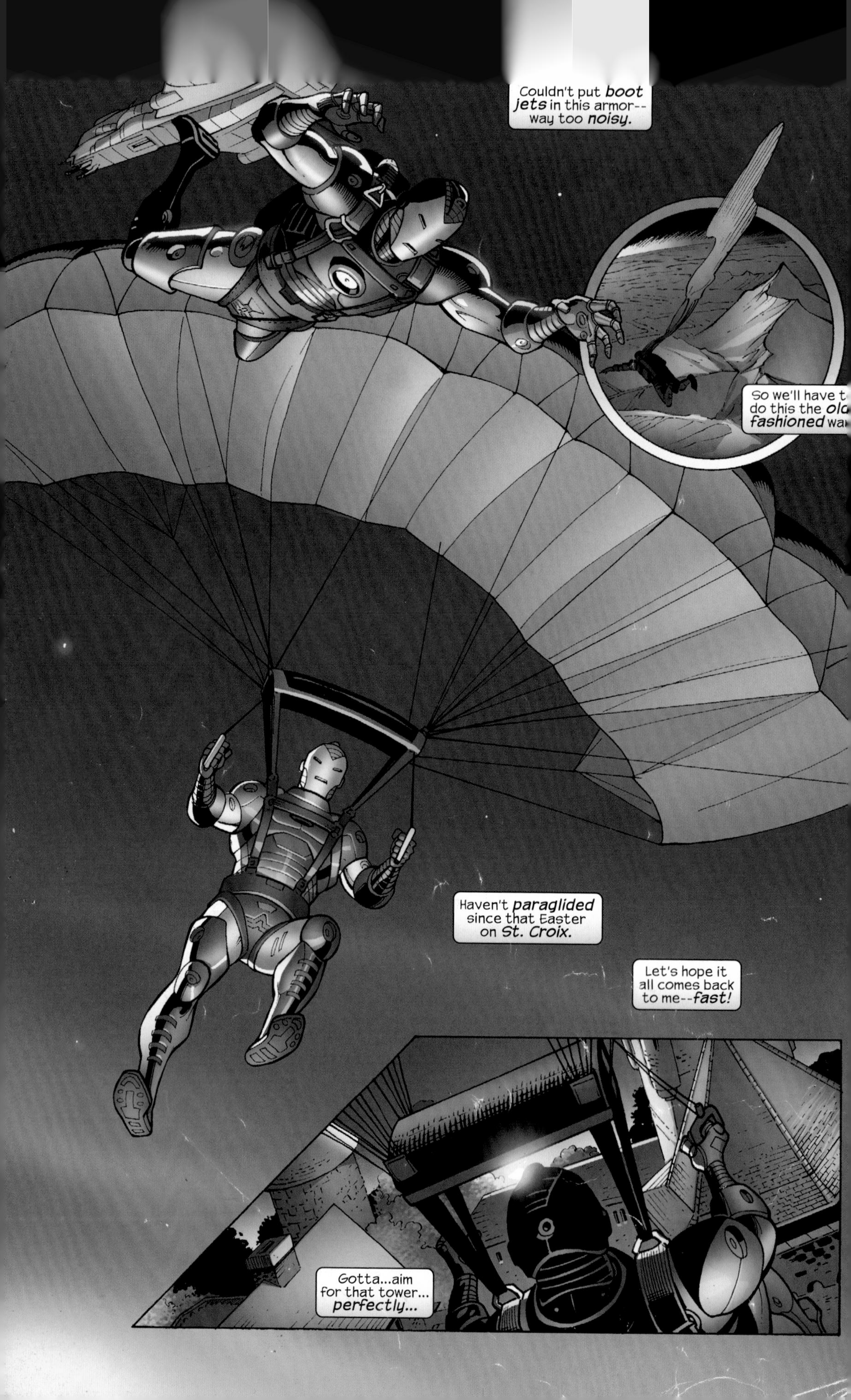
Couldn't put boot jets in this armor-- way too noisy.
So we'll have t do this the old fashioned wa
Haven't paraglided since that Easter on St. Croix.
Let's hope it all comes back to me--fast!
Gotta...aim for that tower... perfectly...

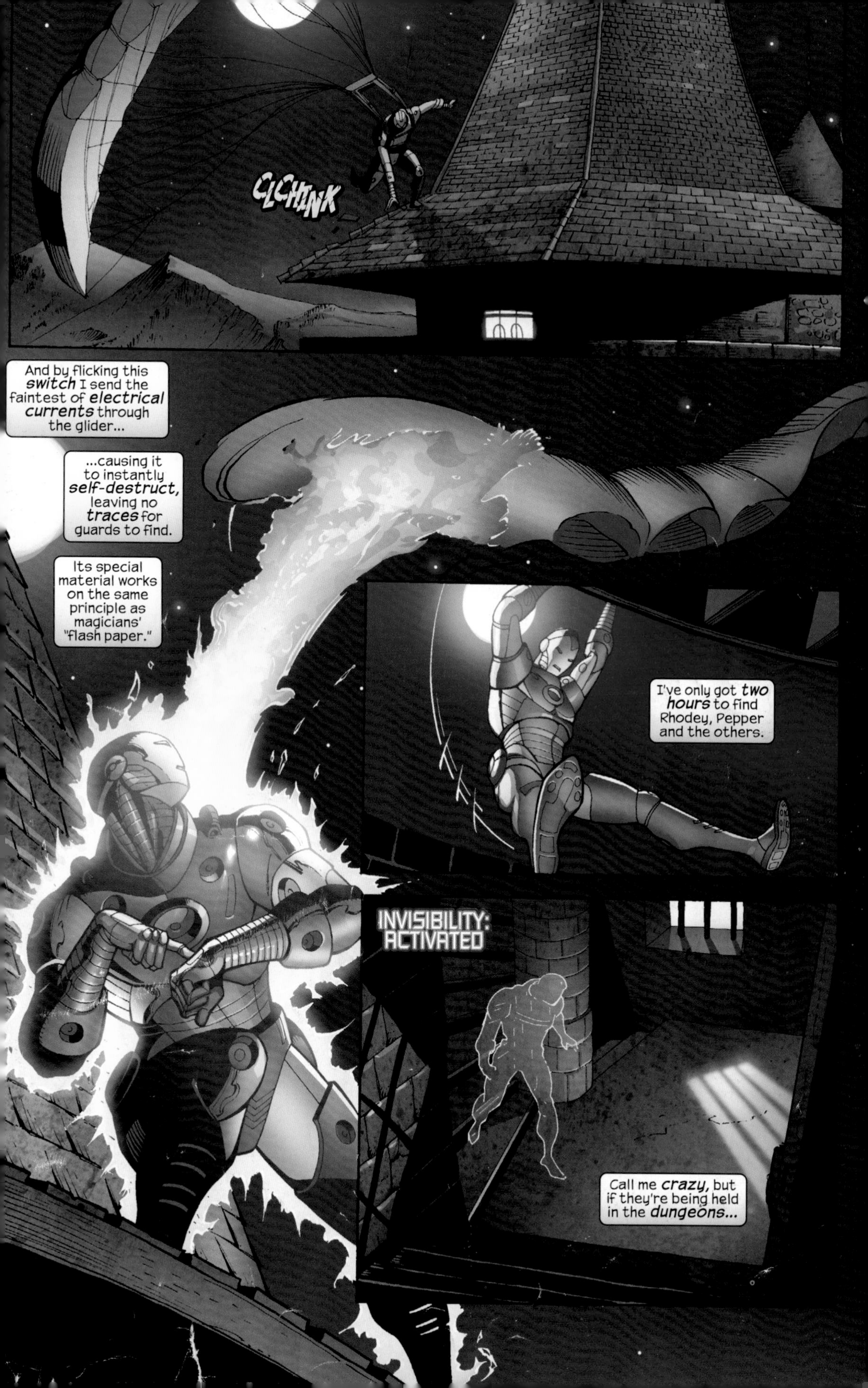
CLCHINK
And by flicking this switch I send the faintest of electrical currents through the glider...
...causing it to instantly self-destruct, leaving no traces for guards to find.
Its special material works on the same principle as magicians' "flash paper."
I've only got two hours to find Rhodey, Pepper and the others.
INVISIBILITY: ACTIVATED
Call me crazy, but if they're being held in the dungeons...

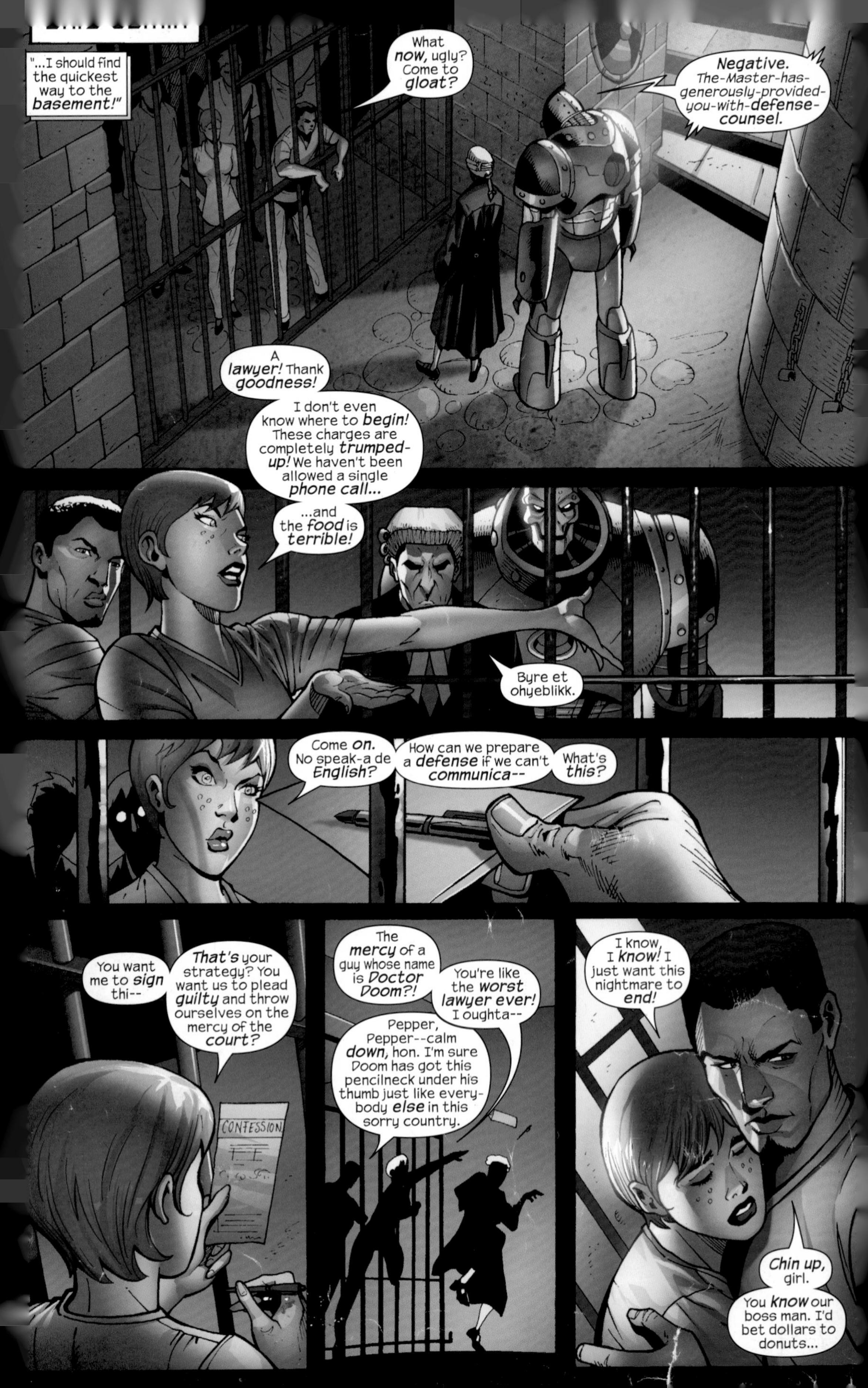
"...I should find the quickest way to the basement!"
What now, ugly? Come to gloat?
Negative. The-Master-has-generously-provided-you-with-defense-counsel.
A lawyer! Thank goodness!
I don't even know where to begin! These charges are completely trumped-up! We haven't been allowed a single phone call...
...and the food is terrible!
Byre et ohyeblikk.
Come on. No speak-a de English?
How can we prepare a defense if we can't communica--
What's this?
You want me to sign thi--
That's your strategy? You want us to plead guilty and throw ourselves on the mercy of the court?
CONFESSION
The mercy of a guy whose name is Doctor Doom?!
You're like the worst lawyer ever! I oughta--
Pepper, Pepper--calm down, hon. I'm sure Doom has got this pencilneck under his thumb just like everybody else in this sorry country.
I know, I know! I just want this nightmare to end!
Chin up, girl.
You know our boss man. I'd bet dollars to donuts...

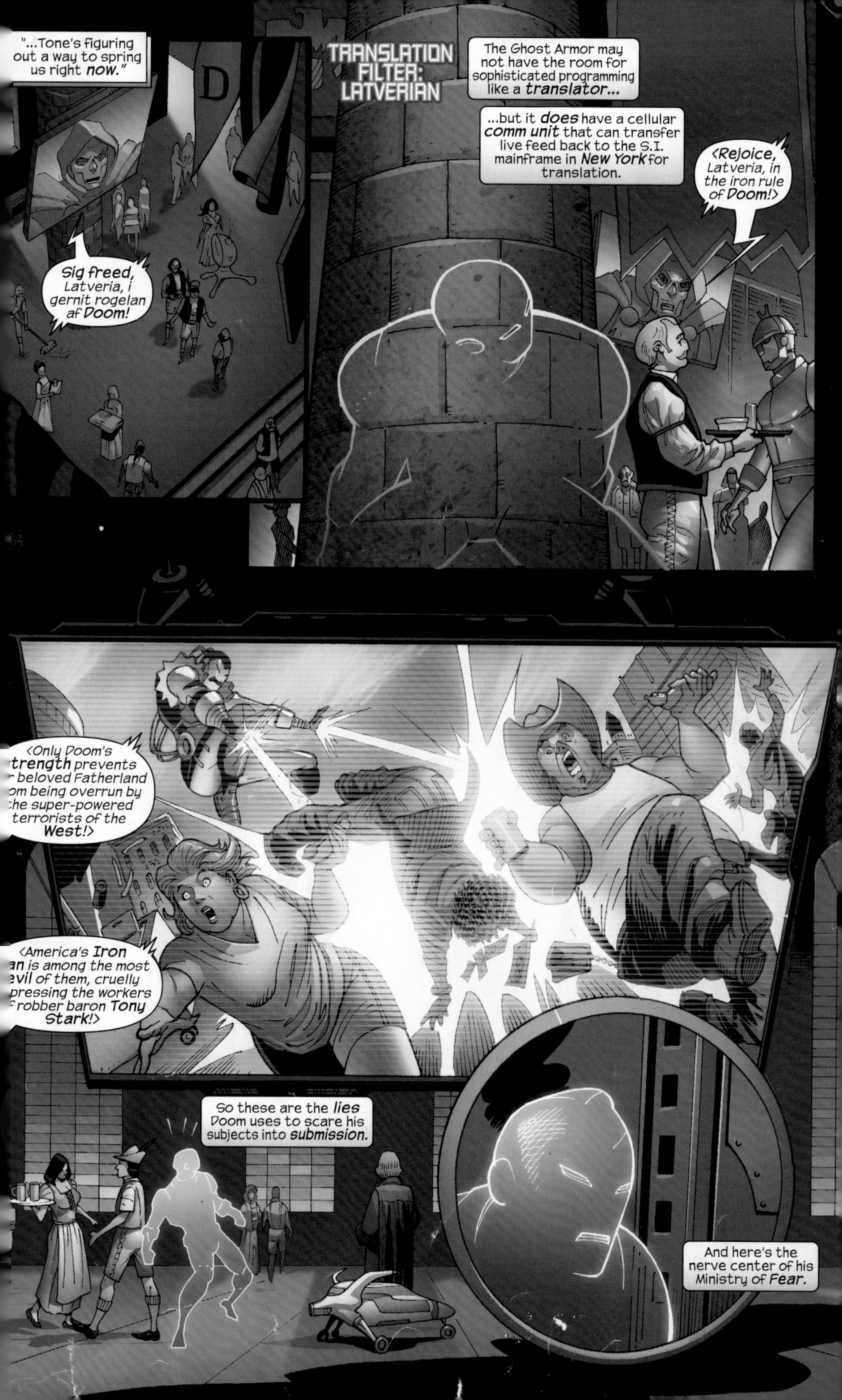
"...Tone's figuring out a way to spring us right now."
TRANSLATION FILTER: LATVERIAN
The Ghost Armor may not have the room for sophisticated programming like a translator...
...but it does have a cellular comm unit that can transfer live feed back to the S.I. mainframe in New York for translation.
Sig freed, Latveria, i gernit rogelan af Doom!
<Rejoice, Latveria, in the iron rule of Doom!>
<Only Doom's strength prevents r beloved Fatherland om being overrun by the super-powered terrorists of the West!>
<America's Iron an is among the most evil of them, cruelly pressing the workers robber baron Tony Stark!>
So these are the lies Doom uses to scare his subjects into submission.
And here's the nerve center of his Ministry of Fear.

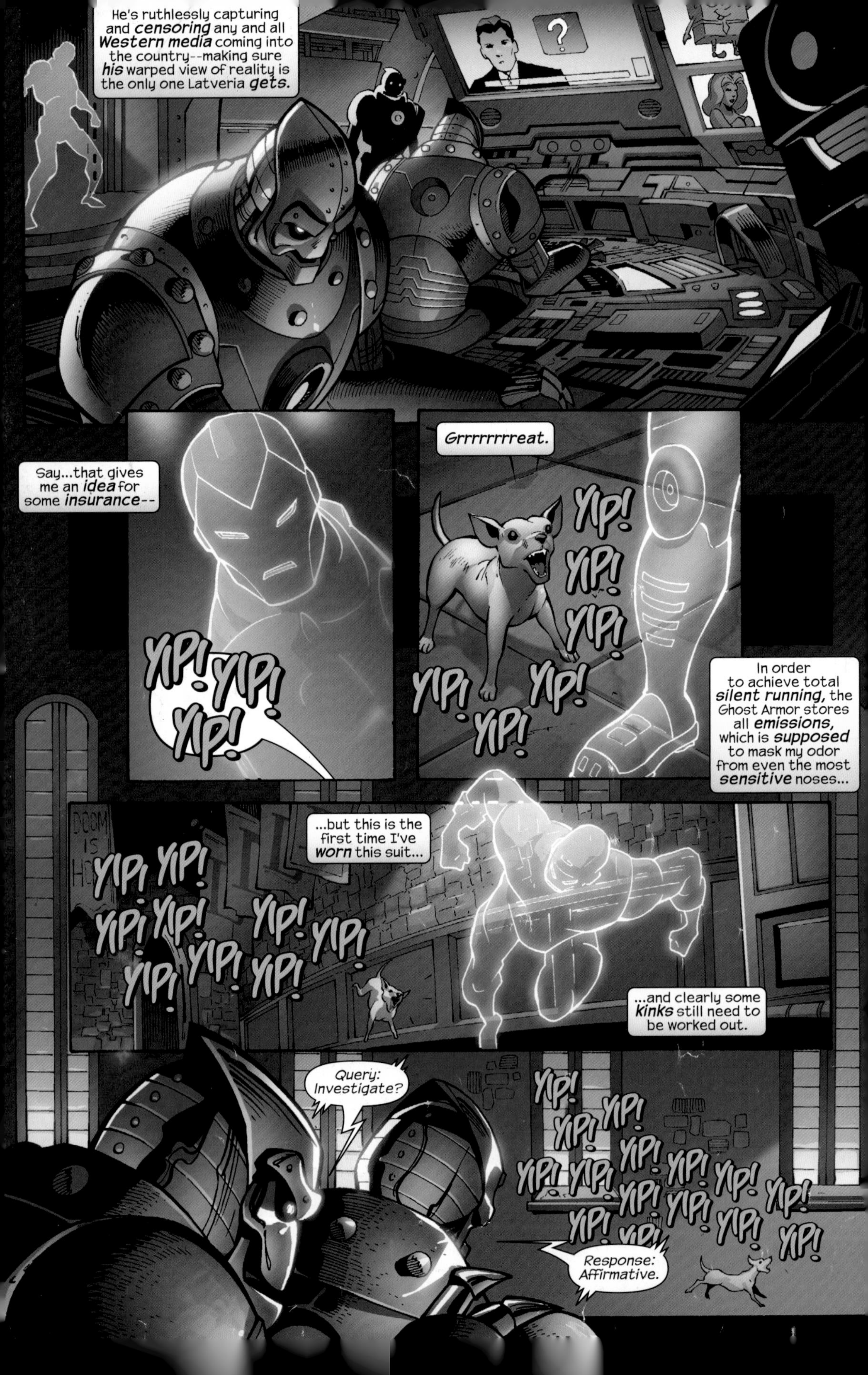
He's ruthlessly capturing and censoring any and all Western media coming into the country--making sure his warped view of reality is the only one Latveria gets.
?
Say...that gives me an idea for some insurance--
YIP! YIP! YIP!
Grrrrrrrreat.
YIP! YIP! YIP! YIP! YIP! YIP!
In order to achieve total silent running, the Ghost Armor stores all emissions, which is supposed to mask my odor from even the most sensitive noses...
...but this is the first time I've worn this suit...
DOOM IS
YIP! YIP! YIP! YIP! YIP! YIP! YIP! YIP! YIP!
...and clearly some kinks still need to be worked out.
Query: Investigate?
YIP! YIP! YIP! YIP! YIP! YIP! YIP! YIP! YIP! YIP! YIP! YIP! YIP! YIP! YIP!
Response: Affirmative.

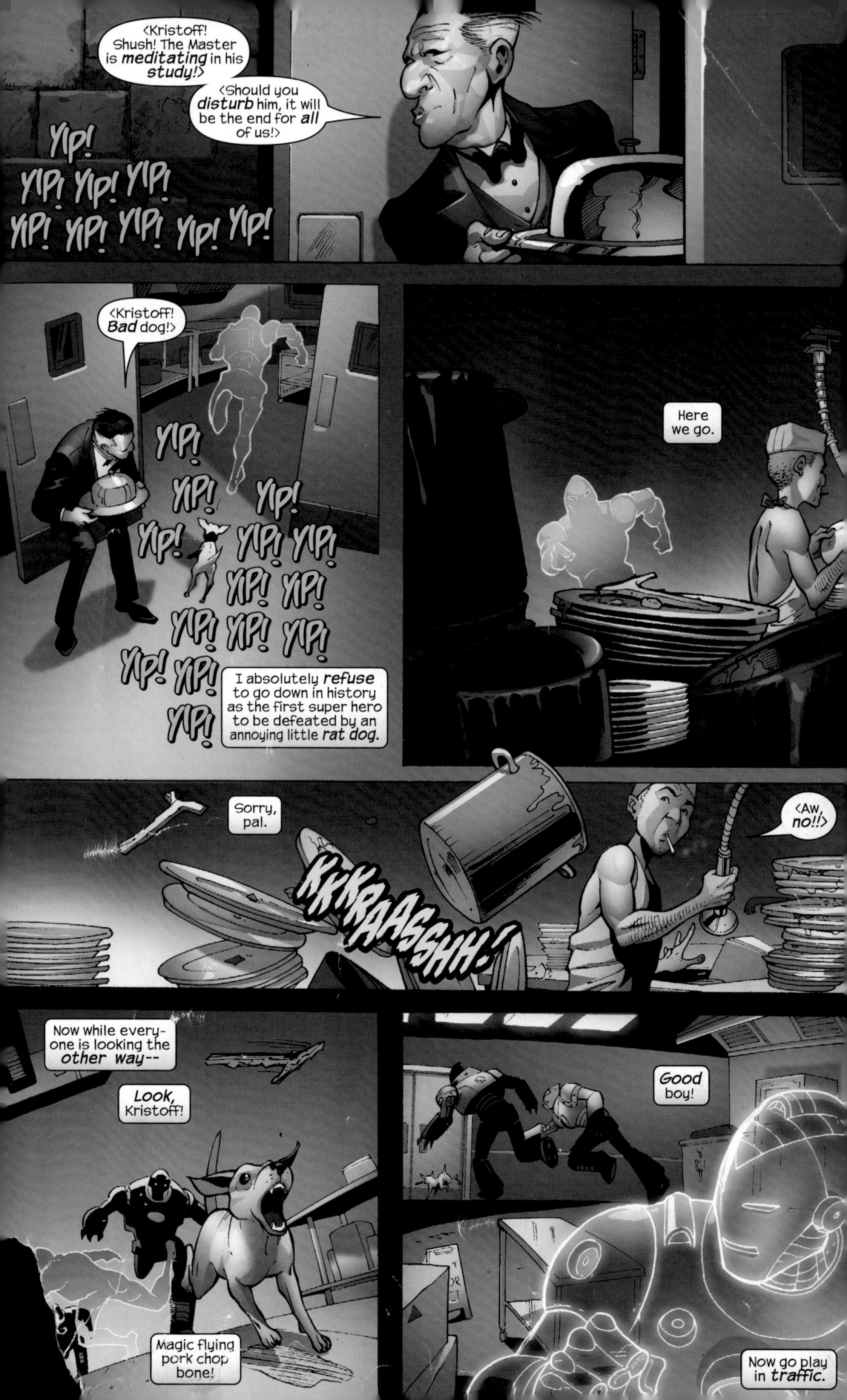

<Kristoff! Shush! The Master is *meditating* in his *study!*>
<Should you *disturb* him, it will be the end for *all* of us!>
YIP! YIP! YIP! YIP! YIP! YIP! YIP! YIP! YIP!
<Kristoff! *Bad* dog!>
YIP! YIP! YIP! YIP! YIP! YIP! YIP! YIP! YIP! YIP! YIP! YIP! YIP!
I absolutely *refuse* to go down in history as the first super hero to be defeated by an annoying little *rat dog.*
Here we go.
Sorry, pal.
KKKRAASSHH!
<Aw, *no!!*>
Now while every-one is looking the *other way--*
Look, Kristoff!
Magic flying pork chop bone!
Good boy!
Now go play in *traffic.*

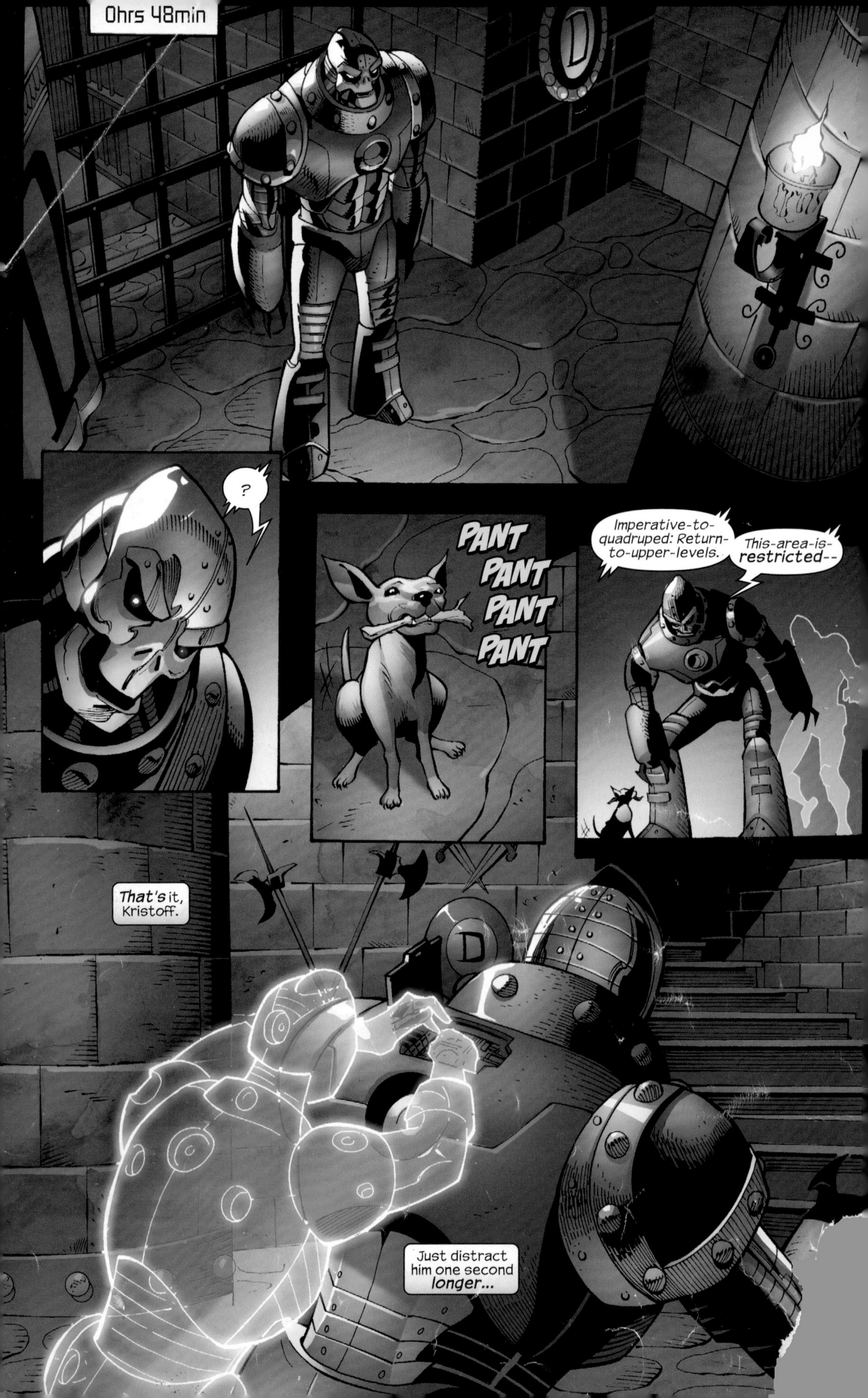

0hrs 48min
?
PANT PANT PANT PANT
Imperative-to-quadruped: Return-to-upper-levels.
This-area-is-restricted--
That's it, Kristoff.
Just distract him one second longer...

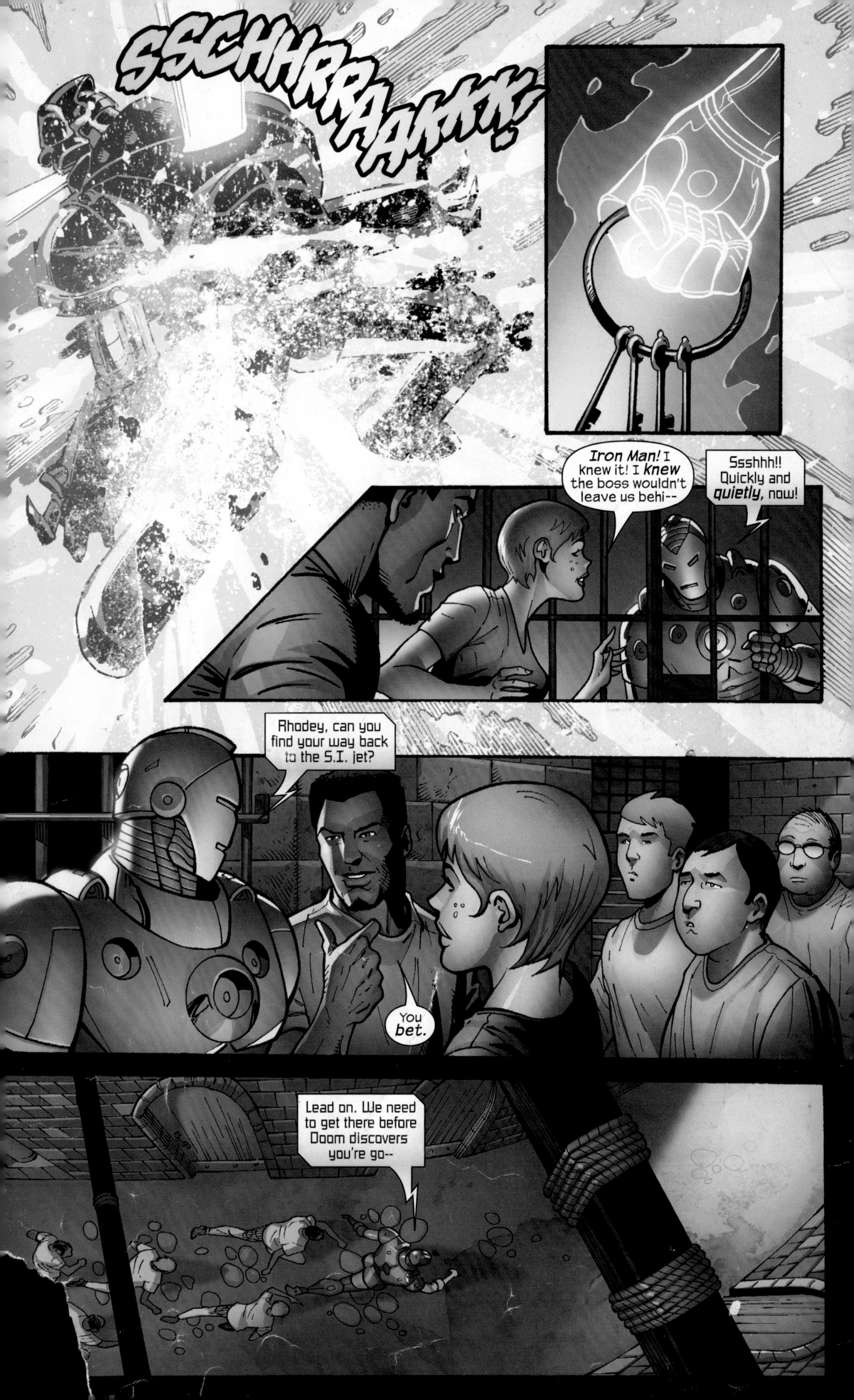
SSCHHRRAAKKK!
Iron Man! I knew it! I knew the boss wouldn't leave us behi--
Ssshhh!! Quickly and quietly, now!
Rhodey, can you find your way back to the S.I. jet?
You bet.
Lead on. We need to get there before Doom discovers you're go--

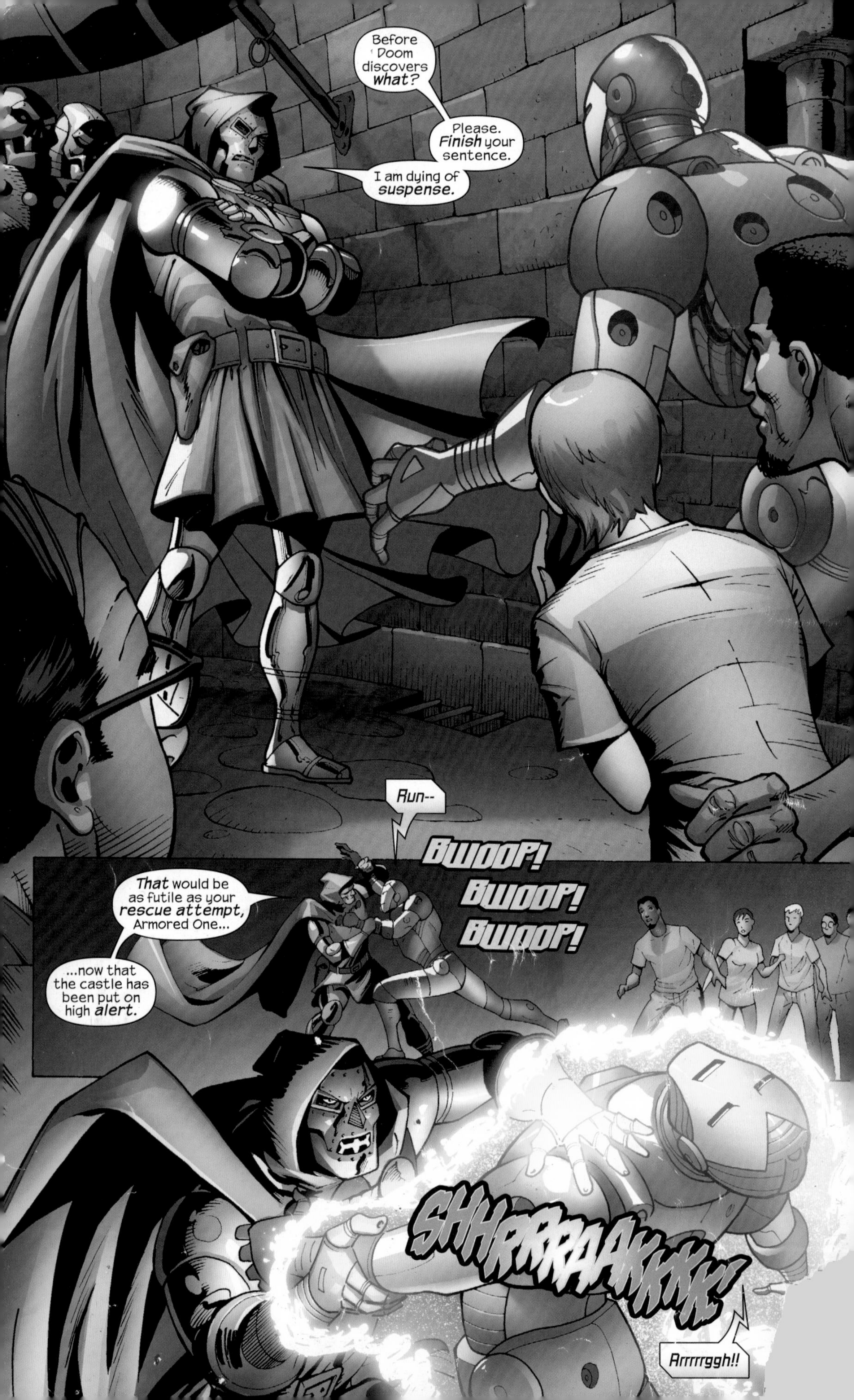
Before Doom discovers what?
Please. Finish your sentence.
I am dying of suspense.
Run--
BWOOP! BWOOP! BWOOP!
That would be as futile as your rescue attempt, Armored One...
...now that the castle has been put on high alert.
SHHRRRAAKKKK!
Arrrrrggh!!

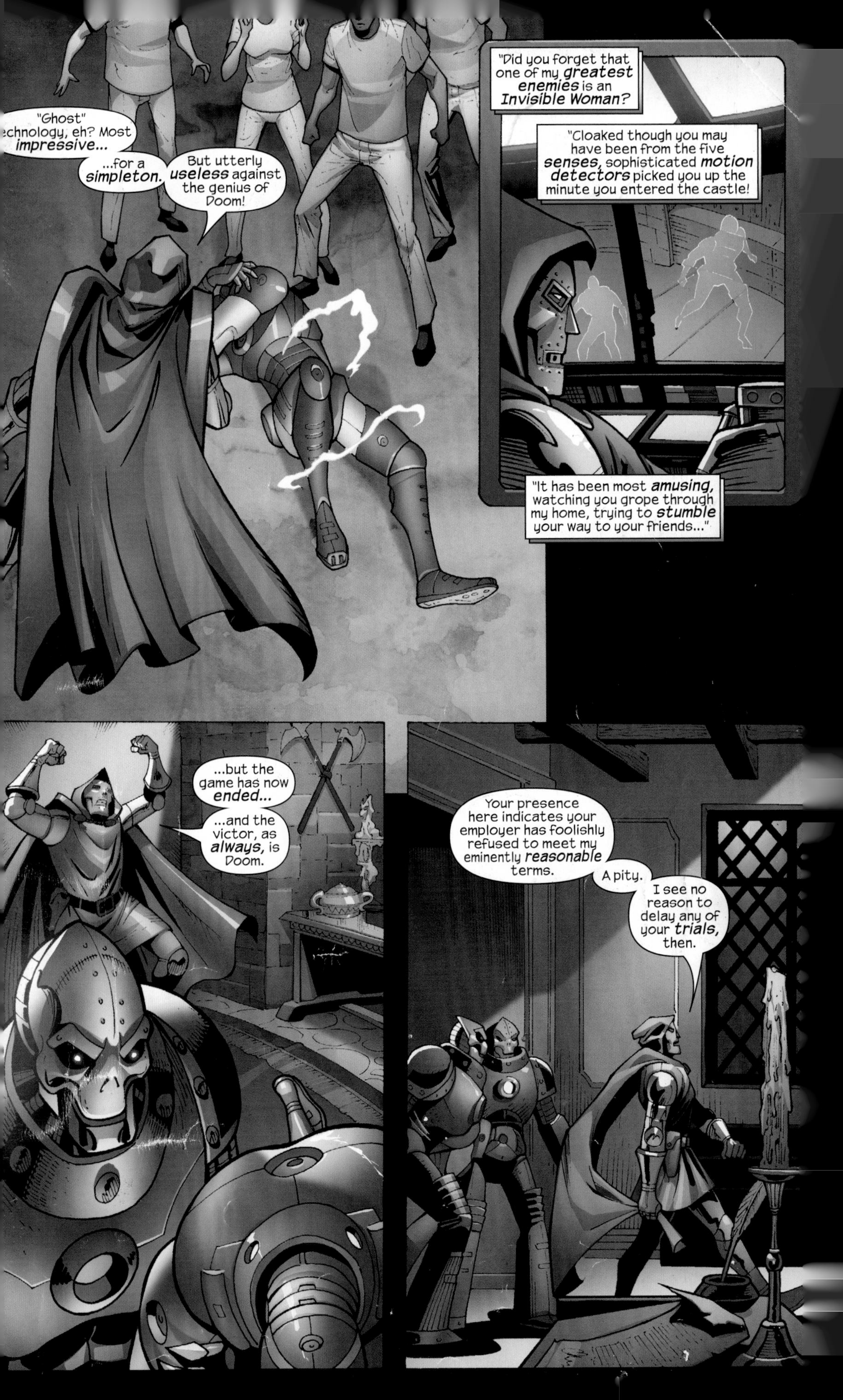

"Ghost" echnology, eh? Most impressive...
...for a simpleton.
But utterly useless against the genius of Doom!
"Did you forget that one of my greatest enemies is an Invisible Woman?
"Cloaked though you may have been from the five senses, sophisticated motion detectors picked you up the minute you entered the castle!
"It has been most amusing, watching you grope through my home, trying to stumble your way to your friends..."
...but the game has now ended...
...and the victor, as always, is Doom.
Your presence here indicates your employer has foolishly refused to meet my eminently reasonable terms.
A pity.
I see no reason to delay any of your trials, then.

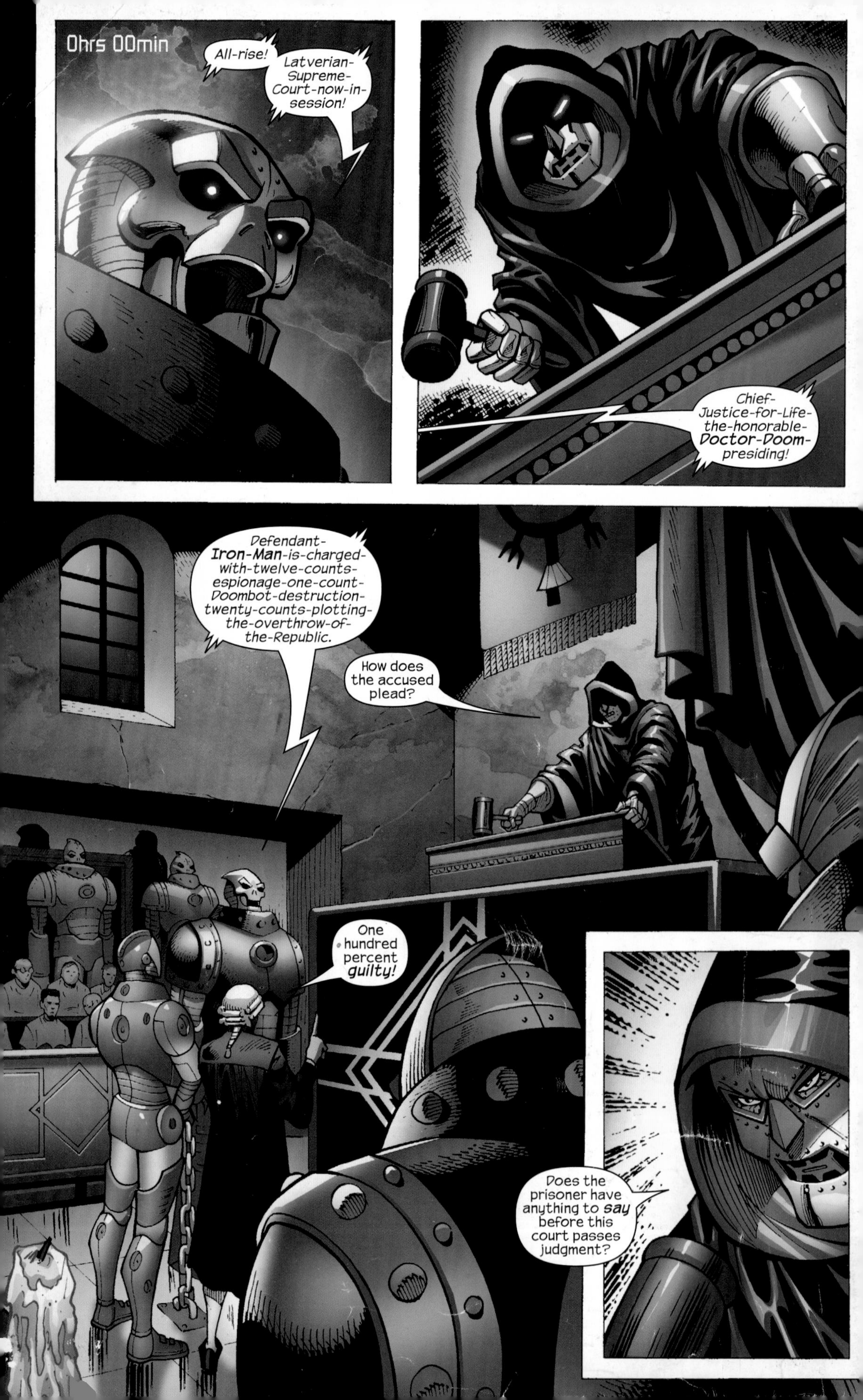

0hrs 00min
All-rise!
Latverian-Supreme-Court-now-in-session!
Chief-Justice-for-Life-the-honorable-Doctor-Doom-presiding!
Defendant-Iron-Man-is-charged-with-twelve-counts-espionage-one-count-Doombot-destruction-twenty-counts-plotting-the-overthrow-of-the-Republic.
How does the accused plead?
One hundred percent guilty!
Does the prisoner have anything to say before this court passes judgment?

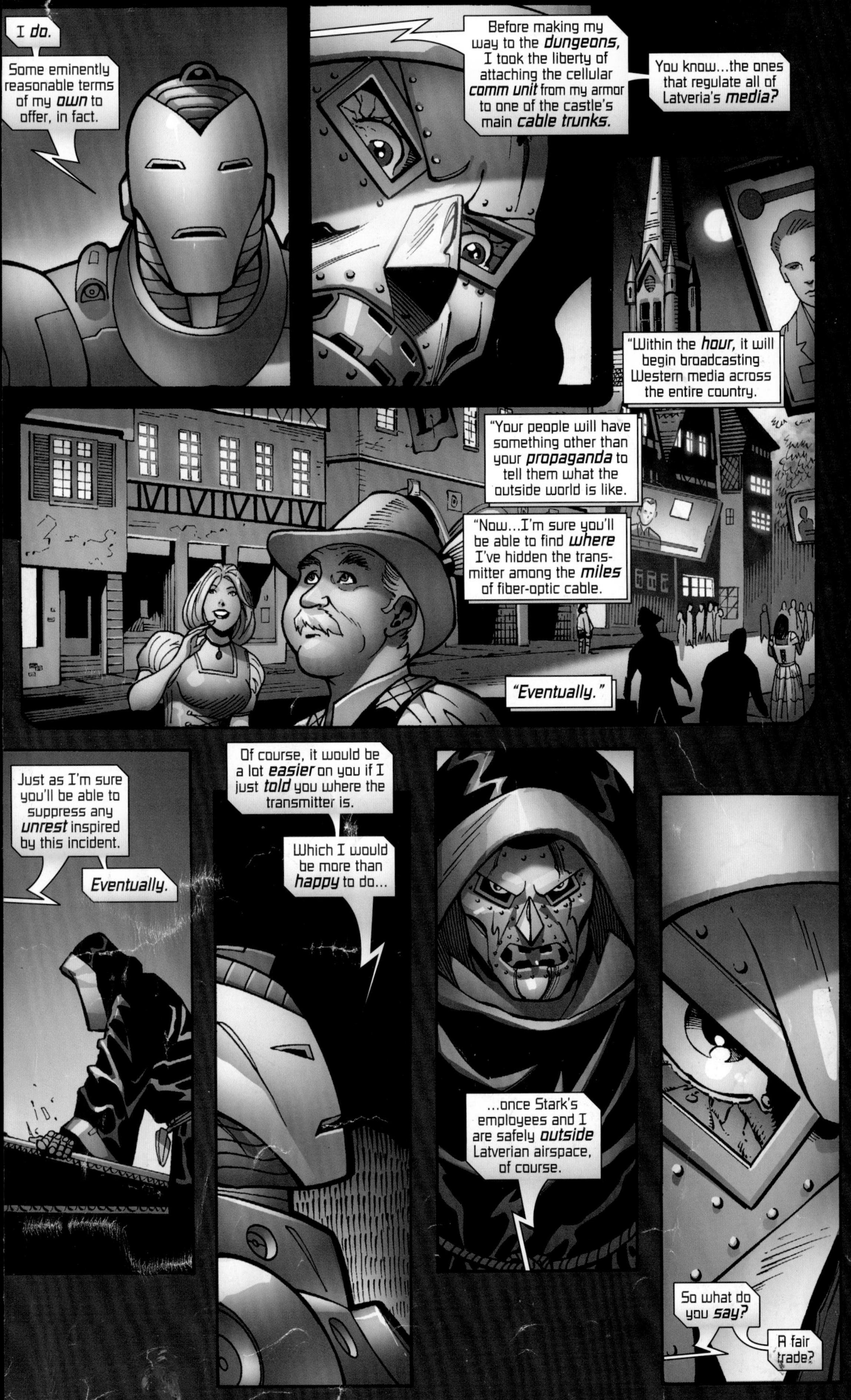

I do.
Some eminently reasonable terms of my own to offer, in fact.
Before making my way to the dungeons, I took the liberty of attaching the cellular comm unit from my armor to one of the castle's main cable trunks.
You know...the ones that regulate all of Latveria's media?
"Within the hour, it will begin broadcasting Western media across the entire country.
"Your people will have something other than your propaganda to tell them what the outside world is like.
"Now...I'm sure you'll be able to find where I've hidden the transmitter among the miles of fiber-optic cable.
"Eventually."
Just as I'm sure you'll be able to suppress any unrest inspired by this incident.
Eventually.
Of course, it would be a lot easier on you if I just told you where the transmitter is.
Which I would be more than happy to do...
...once Stark's employees and I are safely outside Latverian airspace, of course.
So what do you say?
A fair trade?

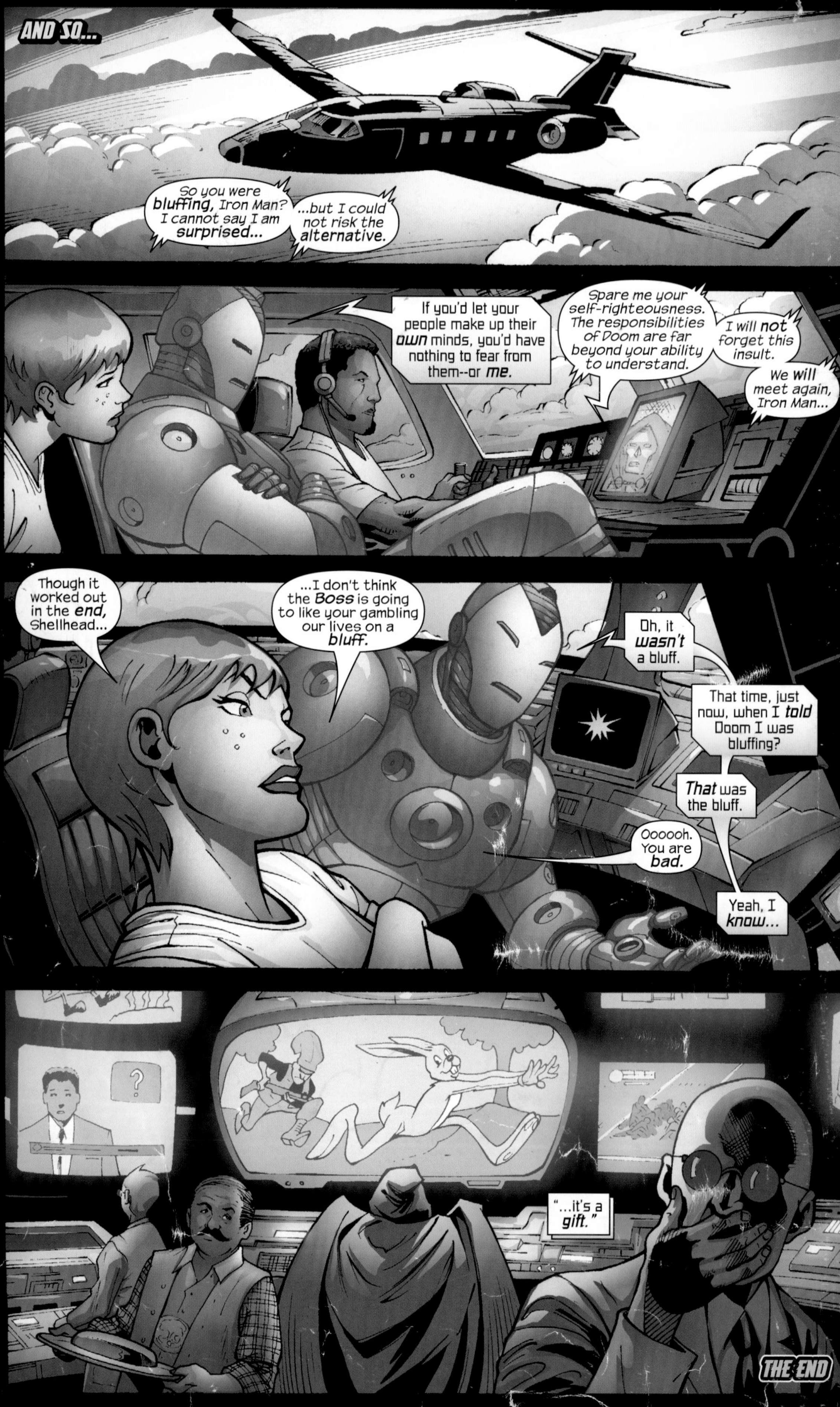
AND SO...
So you were bluffing, Iron Man? I cannot say I am surprised...
...but I could not risk the alternative.
If you'd let your people make up their own minds, you'd have nothing to fear from them--or me.
Spare me your self-righteousness. The responsibilities of Doom are far beyond your ability to understand.
I will not forget this insult.
We will meet again, Iron Man...
Though it worked out in the end, Shellhead...
...I don't think the Boss is going to like your gambling our lives on a bluff.
Oh, it wasn't a bluff.
That time, just now, when I told Doom I was bluffing?
That was the bluff.
Oooooh. You are bad.
Yeah, I know...
"...it's a gift."
THE END